Hotwife In The Strip Club - A Wife watching Hot Wife Turned Stripper Open Relationship Romance Novel

Karly Violet

Published by Karly Violet, 2021.

This is a work of fiction. Similarities to real people, places, or events are entirely coincidental.

HOTWIFE IN THE STRIP CLUB - A WIFE WATCHING HOT WIFE TURNED STRIPPER OPEN RELATIONSHIP ROMANCE NOVEL

First edition. October 11, 2021.

Copyright © 2021 Karly Violet.

ISBN: 979-8201540982

Written by Karly Violet.

Hotwife In The Strip Club
A Wife Watching Hot Wife Turn Stripper
Open Relationship Romance Novel

All Right Reserved © Karly Violet 2021
All rights reserved. No part of this publication may be reproduced, distributed, or transmitted in any form or by any means without the prior written permission of the author, except in the case of brief quotations embodied in critical reviews and certain noncommercial uses permitted by copyright law.
Individuals on the cover are models and are used for illustrative purposes only.

Author's note: All character in this story are 18 years of age and older. This is a work of fiction, any resemblance to real live name or events are purely coincidental.

Be aware: This story is written for, and should only be enjoyed by, ADULTS. It includes explicit descriptions of intense sexual activity between consenting adults.

Note that this work of fiction resembles a fantasy world, all events taking place are a result of a role play amongst all parties and all parties are fully consenting adults.

This ebook should be purchased/borrowed by and read by adults only.

Chapter One: An Avalanche of Bills

There are times from week to week when we feel so desperate for money that I contemplate robbing a bank. Though thoughts run through my mind of how I could do such a thing, I know better than to ever try to carry out the action. It's far more likely that I would be caught and sent to a federal prison rather than profit at all from whatever cash I could get from a teller's drawers. Even so, it has been a tempting thought to entertain on occasion.

"Another late notice," I lament as I look over at my wife, Lindsey. "We owe so much in late fees that it's equal to a damned car payment this month.

My wife nods her head in somber agreement as she swirls a spoon in her coffee. "There's more month than money sometimes." She looks over at me and smiles. "I'll be working extra shifts at the day spa over the next couple of weeks, so maybe that will help some with the bills."

I love my beautiful wife. At five-feet-seven, she's an athletic goddess. Lindsey played volleyball in college and even aspired to run track in the Olympics at one time. Though she didn't make it on the team, she did show very well and one of the track judges suggested she try again in four years. Somehow, I think our current situation will steal away from her ability to effectively train, though. More hours of work for her means less time for her to run in her time off.

"I'm sorry that you have to do that," I reply. "Business has been down at the shop and we are trying to drum up some more customers in the near future. If I had just taken that fucking job..." My voice trails off as I think about an opportunity I turned down with a company in our area just last year. They approached me to ask if I would be willing to work as their local network engineer, and my pride told them that I wasn't interested. It would have meant seventy thousand dollars per year, with benefits. Instead, I find myself scraping by with my partner at a computer repair shop that we own together.

"You would have hated that job," Lindsey points out. "We both would have hated what it would have meant for you. You have always dreamed of being your own boss, and now you are. Sure, it means that there will be some lean times, but I can see where things will probably get better for us in the future, Braden. Just keep your chin up." My wife smiles at me, her dark brown eyes looking intensely into mine.

Smiling back at her, I ask, "So, have you looked into the hand job thing at the spa?"

Lindsey laughs. "Seriously? You're going to bring that up again? I've told you before, it's not that kind of day spa. We do the whole massage and therapy thing, but no hanky panky with the clients."

"You would be great at it," I chuckle. "Think of it. You could give some guy a nice back run and then when he flips over with a hardon you can just rub him off. It might be worth an extra few dollars."

"And a trip to jail," she replies. "Besides, I don't massage people, Braden. I'm not a licensed massage therapist."

"But you're great at giving hand jobs," I insist with a laugh.

"Ninety percent of our clientele are women. *Older* women."

"You can help them get off too." We both begin to laugh as I sit back in my chair at the dining room table. Looking at the bills this morning has gotten me a little punch-drunk and willing to say or do anything to simply forget our current problems.

"I can help you," Lindsey says to me as she moves around in her seat and reaches for my shorts. My wife moves her hand through the leg of my shorts and pulls out my hardening cock. Her hand begins to move slowly up and down as her fingers work over the tip of it.

"Holy shit, baby," I moan as she plays with me.

"You're horny. That's why you are talking about happy endings, Braden. I've been neglecting you a little, haven't I?" She smiles at me, her shoulder-length brown hair sitting to one side as she tilts her head so that she can get a better view of her handiwork.

"You're going to make me come in a minute, Lindsey. You know that, right?"

She smiles. "I would be disappointed if you didn't." Her soft hand keeps massaging my long shaft and I begin to grind my ass into the seat. Lindsey excels at anything she does sexually with me and I love her for it. Whether it's a hand job or a blow job, I'm never left feeling like my wife didn't do her best for me. She's a caring lover and I can only hope to be as much for her.

"Honey," I groan as I lean back in the chair and grip the sides of the table. "Fuck, I can't hold it for long."

"Come for me, Braden. Show me what you've got. Make it messy. I'll catch it, sweetie." Her hand moves a little faster now, my balls aching to release their juicy contents. It's been a few days since we have been intimate together, not because of a lack of willingness, but because of our work schedules. Lindsey and I have just been too busy to do much together in the bedroom.

"Shit...*uhhhh...*" The first spurt from my cock is powerful and strikes the edge of the table as my wife smiles from ear to ear. *"Uhhhh...OHHHHH!!!"* Again and again I launch my milky man gravy, her hand tugging at me and helping to drain my balls. *"Fuck...OHHHH...fuck..."* Lindsey stays with me as my body undulates and I finish my orgasm. I feel terrible that I haven't given her as much this morning as she has given me.

"That was messy," my wife says with a giggle. "Nice job, big guy."

"Damn, honey." I take a deep breath and then laugh as she reaches for a napkin and wipes my wet shaft for me.

"You have needed that for a while. Maybe you'll have a better day now that you've gotten off." Lindsey winks at me as she gets up from her seat and goes to the laundry basket nearby where she tosses the spunk-laden napkin.

"I owe you now," I say with a smile. "Want to serve me a little breakfast? Maybe a breakfast taco?"

Lindsey shakes her head and giggles. "You're a mess, Braden." She walks back over to me and bends down. We kiss for a moment, our tongues moving in and out of each other's mouths. There's nothing like the way my wife gives a hand job or kisses me. My wife means it whenever she physically interacts with me, and I love it.

"Still," I say as she sits back down in her chair, "I think you could do very well if you were to decide to begin giving people happy endings. Whether they be men or women."

"And you just came," she laughs. "Braden, don't you ever quit?"

"Nah. I just keep going and going." We laugh together for a moment, but soon I begin to once again feel the pain of despair over our bills. "I've got to find more work for the shop soon or we're going to sink, Lindsey. No matter what, that's a fact."

Sighing, she replies, "Remember, there's light at the end of the tunnel. The manager's position could open up at the day spa in the next few months when Lizzie will be having her baby. I would make double the pay and that should help to cover things. Have faith, Braden." My wife reaches for her cup and takes a sip of coffee. Though she seems confident that our financial worries will lessen in time, I am not. We are a month past due on our house payment, more than two months late on some credit cards, and we are being threatened by those who have grown tired of our late payment habits. The constant barrage of phone calls and collection letters is beginning to wear heavily on me.

"I hope things work out like you say they will. If they do, kudos to us. If not...well, let's just not go there."

"We're not filing for bankruptcy, Braden. Get that thought out of your head. I would rather have to go to court over our debt and work out some arrangement instead of doing that." Lindsey reaches over and puts her hand on mine. "Please don't worry so much, sweetheart. We'll be okay. We always have been."

It's a constant concern of mine that my wife and I are both thirty years old but our bank account looks more like a university student's. Why are we so financially behind when we both work hard, long hours? Don't we deserve to finally get caught up? I'm good with having to go paycheck to paycheck in order to pay our bills, but the constant late notices and fees are beginning to stack up.

"I love you, baby. You're right. I need to just keep my mind on what we are doing right now and what we have planned for the future. Things will get better one day." I say this for my wife's benefit more than mine. It's difficult for me to completely believe a word of it.

"We will." Lindsey gets up and kisses me again. "I've got to get ready for work. I'll see you tonight?"

"Yeah, tonight. I'll cook tonight."

"I appreciate that." My wife smiles and turns to go to the bedroom and get dressed for work. I have another hour before I plan to leave, so I sit back and just stare at the table covered in bills and notices. Maybe she's right. Maybe things will get better soon. I hope so. There's not much more of this that I can take.

Chapter Two: Collection Notice

"Hey, buddy!" Jeff smiles at me as I walk into our computer repair shop.

"Morning. Sorry I'm a few minutes late." I put down a laptop computer I took home to work on last night. If only I could make overtime pay for this sort of work.

"Yeah, the rush hour was hell around here." A smirk rides across my partner's face before he breaks out laughing. "Honestly, I would have been happy to have seen a half-dozen or so new customers walk through our doors." My business partner has been my best friend for the better part of twenty years. We met in elementary school and even attended a local university together. His degree is in computer graphics while mine is in computer engineering. We make an interesting duo as we struggle to make the bills here in our small shop.

"The new laptop from that one Chinese company is out."

"Ah, the Xao Delta Pro," Jeff replies. "A real piece of workmanship."

"A real piece of shit," I laugh. "I've been reading up on some of the computer repair forums and they say that for the three-grand price tag, it performs like a cheap Walmart laptop. It's got something to do with one of the processors being far too underpowered for the machine."

"Let's hope that it brings us some more work," Jeff says as he looks over an iPad. "We need a steady influx of shitty computers to keep the lights on around here." I laugh along with him as I watch what he's doing.

"Jeff, what's going on with that iPad?"

He shrugs his shoulders. "A lady brought it in this morning and she said the power button doesn't work every time. I've been turning it off and then back on without a problem for the last half-hour, though." My partner hands it over to me and I begin to look it over.

"It could be a worn contact in the switch," I tell him as I turn it off and then back on. "That happens a lot."

"And it's cheap to fix," Jeff says with a frown. "Dammit."

"Around fifty dollars for the part. I mean, it's not a difficult repair at all and she can come back to get it later in the day." After turning it off for a second time, I turn the iPad onto its side and try to turn it back on.

Then, smiling, I point it out to Jeff. "It won't turn on if it's on its side like this. It's a worn button pad. Easy fix."

"Shit." Jeff frowns as he sits back in his stool chair. "I was hoping it would be a five-hundred-dollar thingy."

"This iPad isn't even worth that much money," I laugh. After putting it down, I tell him, "This is the way we can earn future business, though. We don't overcharge and we fix the exact problem. The lady will be happy that she has a working iPad power button again and we'll have gained a future customer and possibly some useful word of mouth from her to her friends."

Jeff nods, though reluctantly. "The word of mouth thing hasn't been working out all that well for us recently, but I suppose you're right. Maybe if they all buy the Xao laptop we'll get a little more business."

"Yeah, I hope so." Sighing, I ask, "Did the electric bill get paid?" Jeff does the financial end of things for our little business since his repair capabilities are limited.

"It did. Just barely, but yes."

"Things are sucking here too," I say with a grimace. "My own bills are starting to pile up and give my wife and I a headache."

"Is your wife still at the day spa?" he asks.

"She's still there. At least, for now. Even though it started out as a temporary gig for her, Lindsey is eyeing the manager's position in a few months. It would pay a lot more than what she is making right now."

"That's good," Jeff replies. "I'm sorry that you're both having money troubles, though. I can help out a little if you would like."

"No, I don't take charity," I reply.

"It's not charity," Jeff insists. "It would be a loan from me to you both. You can pay it back over time."

"We already have too many of those," I tell him with a grunting chuckle. "No, Lindsey and I will be just fine. We just have to get caught up on the bills as soon as we can."

"And running this place hasn't helped, huh?" My partner looks at me with sorrowful eyes. The computer repair shop wasn't originally my idea, but his. Not able to find work as a computer graphics artist in our area, Jeff approached me with the idea of opening the shop. I could be the repair tech and he could be the customer service and finance manager here. Since I was in between jobs, I thought it would be a good move on my part. So, I partnered up with him and we raised the money together. Things went very well at first, but over the last year or so business has been down. More people are either throwing away problematic electronics or trading them in rather than having them repaired by an independent shop. Of course, without Apple's approval to make repairs on their electronics, customers don't necessarily want to give us a chance to fix those items.

"I love working with you, man. Don't ever doubt that." I nod and smile over at Jeff before turning my attention to the other customer electronics we have sitting on a back counter. "I'll get you a list of those machines that are repaired as I get them completed. If you could call those customers, I would appreciate it."

"Not a problem. Just send them my way." My partner turns back toward the front countertop and I begin to work on the iPad. I might as well get this repair finished first thing this morning since it is a quick job. As I work, I hear our front door chime sound out and a man begins to speak loudly with Jeff.

"I want that fucking laptop back if you can't have it finished today!" He looks hard at my partner as he presses his hands on the countertop. "You've had it for three days already."

"Mr. Peters?" I walk up and smile at the angry customer. "How are you doing today?"

"I would be doing a lot better if you guys could get that laptop back to me in a timely manner. I have work to do and I need that computer. Why isn't it finished yet?"

I nod my head in understanding at his frustration. "Mr. Peters, I told you when you brought it in that it could take up to two weeks. We had to order the replacement RAM sticks that are defective in your laptop. They are proprietary and can take some time to get."

"Just put some other sticks inside it. You sell them here, right?" He points at the display we have nearby of a certain brand's RAM sticks.

"We have those, sure, but they aren't made for your particular device. They won't work."

"Then why run a shop at all if you're not prepared?" His bright blue eyes bore into mine as he makes his point. Though I want to tell him to shut the fuck up and let us do our job, I know better. We can't afford to lose even one irritated customer.

"Mr. Peterson, the brand of laptop that you have isn't very common in the United States. It's a model that you got in Germany, right?"

"Yeah."

"Well, the repair parts are also in Germany. Please keep in mind that with these sorts of things, we are on a waiting list to get the parts. Lots of other people own these laptops and have the same issues. They need parts. The company doesn't license out its parts to any other vendors, so we're stuck waiting for the RAM sticks from that company. Honestly, you can take your laptop to another shop, and it might take them even longer to get the parts for you because I already have a relationship with the manufacturer. If you can just be patient a little longer, I would very much appreciate it." I smile at Mr. Peterson before adding, "I will take an extra ten percent off the repair cost for your inconvenience, alright? And I'll personally deliver it back to you as soon as I've completed the repair work."

The customer appears to calm down a bit as he nods his head. "I'm sorry that I got so pissed off. It's just that I don't have any way of working on my personal financial statements without that laptop."

"Is it a program you use that's on the computer or online?" I ask.

"Online," he tells me. I smile and turn to walk to the back counter. I soon return with a laptop.

"This is a loaner laptop you can use for now. Just use the guest tab to log in and then you can work online. Hopefully this will help you out some."

"How much to borrow this?" he asks.

"It's free, Mr. Peterson. I'll pick it up when I deliver your laptop."

He smiles slightly and nods his head. "Thank you for your help. I really do appreciate it." The customer then turns and looks at my partner. "I'm really sorry for being such a jackass. It's been a tough morning for me already."

"Understood. Have a nice day." Jeff and I watch Mr. Peterson leave the store before he turns to look at me. "Another ten percent off? You already promised him twenty percent off, Braden. Where does that leave our bottom line on this repair?"

"Breaking even," I tell him with a frown. "I don't think anything else was going to soothe the savage beast, though. He wanted his fucking laptop now, right? So, it's what I had to do to restore peace." Jeff reluctantly nods his understanding before I turn and go back to my counter in the back of the shop to work.

Times are tough for a lot of people in our area. Mr. Peterson is just one of many business owners who rely on their computers and tablets to get them through the day. I shudder to think that I could suddenly lose my access to the programs I rely upon or the internet services that I need. Though I could be upset with Mr. Peterson's cursing at Jeff, there's really no need to be. We all have difficulties to overcome. His just happens to be a German built laptop that has been blessed with defective RAM sticks.

Chapter Three: Declined

"Hey, honey. I'm in the kitchen," I say as I hear the front door to our home open. Lindsey is home from her long day working at the day spa. She doesn't answer me immediately as she comes in, so I finish what I am doing and walk into the living room to greet her. My wife is sitting on the sofa with a strained look on her face. "What's wrong?"

She looks up at me as her eyes fill with tears. "All I wanted was a fucking soft drink, Braden. Just one two-dollar soft drink. But no, that couldn't happen. Not today. Not any day." Lindsey crosses her arms tightly as she looks down at the floor.

"What happened?" I sit down nearby and take her hand. She's very unhappy and it hurts me deeply to see her like this.

My wife wipes her eyes and then says, "The credit card didn't work at the drive-thru at Burger King. I was on the way home and was so thirsty for something with caffeine in it that I thought I would pull through. Just a soft drink. A fucking Coca-Cola."

"It *declined?"* Lindsey nods her head as she puts a hand over her eyes.

"It was so damned embarrassing, Braden. Those people have seen me come through there before. They know where I work. I pulled up and the card didn't work at all." She takes a breath before adding, "The lady at the window was so rude about the whole ordeal, too. It's as if she thought I had done it on purpose."

"I forgot to pay the bill," I say as I shake my head. "There are so many bills that I forgot that one. I'm sorry, honey. Really I am." I put my arm around my wife and squeeze her tightly as I think about our financial state of affairs. Though it would be easy to blame a soft drink at a drive-thru for this, it's simply a symptom of our dire fiscal situation right now. We can't even make a thirty-dollar minimum payment on a small credit card at this moment.

"I just want to be able to carry some money in my purse or in the car for whenever I need a drink, Braden. Is that so much to ask?"

Shaking my head, I reply, "No, it's not. You should have had that money, baby. It's all my fault."

"It's on both of us," she says as she fights back her tears. "We both make very little money even though we both have college degrees. Why are we scrimping and scraping to get by all the time? What have we done to piss off the heavens?"

I sigh as I stand to my feet. "Come on. Let's eat our dinner before it gets cold. Then we'll take a nice walk to clear our heads." My wife nods her head as she takes my hand and I help her up from the sofa. She has a seat at the dinner table and I go to the kitchen to fill our plates. Thankfully, I was able to find a bag of frozen dinner rolls in the freezer so that our meal will look slightly less pathetic. Even so, it's pretty difficult to dress up macaroni and cheese with Spam.

"Braden," Lindsey says while wincing as I put a plate of the meal in front of her. *"Spam?* Really?"

"I know it's not your favorite thing to eat," I say with a half-smile, "But I seasoned it with some Cavender's. I think you'll find it to taste better than what you've had before." I take a plate to my own seat at the table and sit down beside my wife. "I'm thankful to have this at all. There's not much left in the pantry."

"Spam." Lindsey picks up her fork and digs around at the slice of canned ham bits and then moves her macaroni and cheese around. My wife takes a bite of the Spam, but she then quickly spits the piece out of her mouth. "The texture is awful, Braden. Simply awful. I can't do it. I feel like I'm being a cannibal or something."

"It's not human meat," I tell her. "Please, just try it."

"I don't want it!" Lindsey turns and glares at me. "Dammit, Braden, I don't like Spam. You know that I don't. Why would you cook this shit for me?" She puts her fork down on her plate.

Taking a slow, deep breath, I answer, "It's what we have, my love. You've seen the pantry and the refrigerator. There's nothing in either one of them, but a few crackers and some cans of beans. Would you rather that I served you beans and crackers?"

"Maybe some fucking *steak!*" Lindsey stands to her feet and stomps back to the living room where she once again sits down on the sofa. I put my fork down quietly and get up to follow her.

"I'm sorry," I tell her again. "I didn't really want to make it, but I had no choice." I feel a little deflated that Lindsey has so quickly dismissed what I have made for dinner. It's not prime rib or a half rack of pork ribs, but it's not eating out of a garbage bin either. We will be able to shop for more groceries tomorrow, but only after we each get paid. My wife knows this, and the fact is she tends to be more of an optimist than I.

Lindsey whimpers as she collects her thoughts. "We were better off when we first got married, Braden. During those days, we could afford to go out and get something to eat if we wanted to. It might not have meant getting a fancy meal, but pulling through a drive-thru was never the sort of thing we ever worried about. We knew that we had enough money to do what we had to do back then, but now it's a struggle from one day to the next. What has changed?" She turns her eyes to look at me.

My skin crawls as I realize my wife is accusing me of our financial ills. "That's not fair," I tell her. "You've also taken a pay cut."

"But not as much as yours. You could be doing so much better, Braden. Why are you making less than half what you're worth at a computer shop with Jeff?"

"He's my friend and my partner," I tell her. "You know that Jeff has been good to us. He even offered to lend us some money if we needed any."

"Oh, did he?" Lindsey's eyes narrow. "And you actually thought about doing it, didn't you? Even after my mother offered to give us a little help and you said no."

"Ugh," I say out loud, realizing that it would have probably been much better for me had I kept my mouth shut about Jeff's willingness to help us.

"What is that supposed to mean? My mother would help us if you weren't so stubborn, Braden."

"Help us and put us under her control," I retort. "We have been on the receiving end of your mother's so-called support before, my love. You do remember how she reacted when she gave you a couple of hundred dollars to get a new tire for your car, don't you? I warned you not to tell her that you needed money, but you didn't listen to me."

Lindsey's mother, Jillian, is not a terrible person overall. However, when it comes to her daughter, she can become fanatical about every facet of her life. Even my wife has complained before about the tendrils Jillian will often grow into our relationship if given the chance. It's why I have been so opposed to her asking mommy dearest for any help with our money woes.

"I'm tired of fucking Spam, Braden. I'm tired of not being able to have a fucking soft drink that costs less than two dollars because you forgot to pay a bill. Mother can help us get caught up."

"Dammit, honey," I say with exacerbation. "I'm trying to do what I can to help all this. You told me just this morning that there's light at the end of the tunnel, but now you're so negative. What has changed?"

Lindsey shakes her head while she begins to cry. "They won't hire me for the manager's position after all, Braden. It's been promised to someone else at the day spa." I suddenly realize what this is all about. The same job my wife was hoping to step into a few months from now has been handed to another employee at the spa. It has to feel like a slap in the face for her to have been told this today.

"You're worth more than they pay you," I tell her. "You should try to find something else to do. You have a degree in business administration, after all. Honey, you could be working for one of the bigger companies."

She shakes her head. "My whole resume for the last two years includes working at a fucking spa, Braden. Who in their right mind would see that as being valuable work experience? It's tied me into a very tight niche that I'll have trouble getting out of by applying to another position."

"You could at least try."

Her eyes sharpen on me. "And you could fucking try to go get a real job and stop helping Jeff make a living!" Lindsey gets up and turns before marching toward our bedroom, closing and locking the door behind her. This is definitely not the way I had expected our conversation to go this evening.

I stand up and make my way to the dinner table. Still sitting on the two plates, getting cold, are the slices of Spam and servings of macaroni I had served for both of us. My wife isn't hungry for this, and now neither am I. It's funny how not having enough money for decent food can actually make you feel fuller.

My phone buzzes inside my pocket. It's a text message from Jeff. I open it up to read it. "Hey, that lady with the bad iPad button came in to pick it up just after you left. She was really pleased that it was so cheap to repair. So, she's bringing in her laptop for us to take a look at as well."

"Hopefully we'll make some good money on that repair," I reply in a text before sliding my phone back into my pocket. I pick up the plates on the table and take them to the kitchen. A part of me wants to simply throw the meal out, but I know that would be wasteful and I don't want to do that. So, I put the food into a couple of plastic containers and store them in the refrigerator.

Looking toward our bedroom door, I wonder whether Lindsey will come out at all this evening or if I'm going to find myself banished to the sofa for the night. Though it doesn't happen very often, my wife has seen fit in the past to send me to the living room to sleep. Considering there's no bed in the second bedroom, I suppose I'll have very little options besides a stay in the living room tonight. At least there will be a soccer game on television to watch. It should take my mind off everything that has been happening to us recently.

Chapter Four: Something's Got to Give

I get the feeling that Lindsey wants to tell me something as we walk down the sidewalk in front of some small shops in town. She's quiet today, and she appears to be avoiding eye contact with me. Though I want to know what's going on with her, I decide to play things cool and just let her decide when she wants to finally talk about it.

"It's a nice, breezy day," I say as we make our way past an old fashioned ice cream shop. "Want to go in for a treat?"

"Sure." My wife only briefly looks at me as we turn and walk inside.

Approaching the counter, I ask her, "Do you want the usual? Or maybe something new this time?" This walk has become a sort of habit for us on the weekends when we are both off from work and have just gotten paid. It gives us time to clear the air whenever we need to talk about something as well as to make sure our marital bond is still strong. The couples we have known to get divorced lacked this one feature in their lives.

"I think I want the rocky road this time. Just one scoop, though."

"Just one?" I chuckle. "Well, I think I'm going to be a pig and go for two scoops of the birthday cake ice cream." I nod toward the young woman behind the counter and wait for her to make our treats. Lindsey continues to be painfully silent as she stands beside me.

"Six-fifty-nine," the young server says as she hands us the ice cream cones. I give her eight dollars and tell her to keep the change before going with my wife to a small table near one of the windows. We have a seat and settle down to enjoy the ice cream.

"It's almost too cool outside for ice cream," I note after taking the first lick of ice cream from my cone. "It's a good thing that the sun is out."

"Yeah, it could have been a lot colder." Lindsey smiles at me before licking her own ice cream. Though it is rocky road ice cream, just as she requested, my wife seems to be mostly robotic in the way that she approaches it.

"What is it?" I ask as I look over my own ice cream cone at her. "You have something to say, so go ahead and say it." I offer a smile to let Lindsey know that I'm here for her.

My wife purses her lips together as she looks out the window beside our table. There are undoubtedly thoughts going through her mind as to how to best phrase whatever it is that she wants to tell me. I worry that it could be something that will terribly impact our marriage. After all, Lindsey is a beautiful woman and I have sometimes worried that she might find a better man than me to be with.

"I've been thinking," she begins as she turns her beautiful brown eyes toward me. "I need to do more to bring in money."

"We both do," I agree.

"So, I happened to talk to a friend of mine from college and she reminded me of what she did back then to make a few extra dollars." Lindsey looks out the window again before telling me, "She was a stripper at a nearby gentlemen's club." She stops and looks at me again. "According to her, she could make up to a thousand dollars in one night, and so now she doesn't owe anything for her university studies. She graduated debt free."

I chuckle. "You're debt free from college as well, honey. Thankfully you had scholarships and didn't need to borrow money or go strip for it. That's one payment we don't have to worry about."

"Sure," she replies. "But, there's a gentlemen's club in nearby Abbington. They're looking to hire more strippers."

I raise an eyebrow. "Please tell me that your friend is looking to fill one of those jobs and you're going to tell her about it. I know, Lindsey, that you wouldn't consider working somewhere like that for yourself."

Lindsey looks down at her hands as my heart races inside my chest. My wife, the most beautiful woman in the world as far as I'm concerned, wants to show off her naked body to other men. Where has this idea come from? Sure, her friend worked as a stripper in college, but why is this something Lindsey wants to do now? She's always been extremely modest in the way that she dresses. She rarely wears a bikini to the beach if she knows there will be very many people there.

"Braden, you have to understand that we are in a very difficult situation. I'm afraid that we might lose our home if we don't get things under control very soon." Tears fill her eyes as Lindsey reaches across the table with her free hand and clutches mine. "You do understand, don't you? I have to do this."

"Strip?" I look around the small ice cream shop to make certain there is no one else listening to our conversation. "How can you seriously consider doing something like that? There will be other men looking at your body, Lindsey. There will be some really twisted, perverted freaks watching you gyrate around a fucking pole."

She sighs. "I've already set up an audition at the club for later this afternoon. It's what I want to do to help out with the bills, Braden. You have to let me do this."

I shake my head as I begin to laugh. "No. Absolutely not. You can't do this, honey. I don't want other men ogling your tits and ass." My body shudders at the thought of other men staring at my wife's beautiful breasts and bald muff. I've been to gentlemen's clubs before, so I know what it's like to be one of the audience members. The guys at these things are horny and ready to see or do just about anything sexual. Some will even ask the dancers for sex in the back room. This is not the sort of thing that I want Lindsey to be exposed to.

"I've made up my mind," my wife replies calmly as she looks into my eyes. "Of course, I don't want you there to see me work. I don't want you to see what I'm doing and who sees me doing it. Besides, you can sometimes be the jealous type and the last thing that I need is to have you rail at some guy just because he's stared at me a little too long for your liking." She allows a half-smile before adding, "Just remember that you are the only man for me. Braden, it will be just fine. It's just a job."

"A job." I shake my head again as I bite my lower lip. "A fucking job. Stripping isn't exactly a golden opportunity, babe. There's just too much seediness surrounding that sort of place. There has to be something else we can do besides sell your body."

"It's for only three nights per week, mainly on the weekends. So, it shouldn't really interfere with my job at the day spa. I'll still be bringing in money from there while making money at the club. It's a win-win situation for me, Braden. Hopefully you will come to see it that way as well." She calmly licks at a couple of spots on her ice cream cone where the ice cream has melted and begun to run down. My wife appears to be set on doing this, regardless of my feelings about it.

"Lindsey," I say calmly as I try to sort out my thoughts on what she has proposed to do. "Let's just take a step back and think about this before you go through with it. You say that the interview is this afternoon?"

"Yes," she replies. "In person."

I swallow hard. "You do realize that some guy is going to ask you to strip down in front of him and dance to see if you're what they're looking for, right? Doesn't that bother you just a little?"

Lindsey nods her head. "Sure it bothers me, Braden. But we need this right now. I know I can do this because I'm in such great shape. I can move up and down that bar and hang upside down if I have to." She smiles at me. "Please don't worry, sweetie. I have given this a lot of thought and I want to do it. This could mean a lot more money coming in each week and it might even help us to pay off some of our bills completely. Once we have caught back up, I'll quit that job." My wife leans forward. "And that is exactly what this is, Braden. It's just a *job."* She leans back and licks at her ice cream again.

"Shit." I don't know what I can say at this point to get her to reconsider. Lindsey wants to work in a gentlemen's club to make money to get us out of the fucking debt that is mostly my fault. I'm the one with a degree that could bring in a lot more money. Of course, I would have to abandon my old friend to do so, but wouldn't that be better than letting my wife show off her body to other guys?

"I want to consider this settled," she tells me as she gets up from the table. "And I need to walk by myself for a while. I need to clear my head." Lindsey bends down and gives me a light kiss on the forehead before she adds, "I'll see you at home later. After the interview." My wife turns and walks out of the ice cream shop and I don't bother to try to follow her. She has made up her mind and my presence would only serve to frustrate her.

"This can't be," I say quietly to myself as my ice cream melts and runs down my cone. Though I bought two scoops, I have found that I no longer have an appetite for the sweet concoction. After getting up from my seat, I toss what's left of my ice cream into a trash bin and walk out of the shop. I, too, appear to need to clear my head, so I begin to walk toward the park nearby.

My phone buzzes and I pull it out of my shorts pocket. Answering it, I find a familiar voice on the other end of the call. "Hey, man, what's up?"

"Nothing much," I tell Jeff, my business partner. "What about with you?"

"Well, I have news," he says with a long sigh. "The high school contract we bid on for the repair services? We didn't get it."

"Seriously? I bid just ten percent over our fucking cost. How the hell did we not get it?"

Jeff again sighs. "I think it had to do more with our ability to handle quantity instead of the price when they made the decision. We were definitely the lowest bid, but they were concerned that we couldn't do the repairs quickly enough for them. They went with a larger shop."

"Fuck." I say this loudly enough that a young woman nearby hears me. Our eyes meet for a moment and she frowns at me. I grimace and nod that I understand I shouldn't have been so uncouth in front of her, but then I turn and walk the other way as I continue our conversation. "We're going to be screwed horribly if we can't get a contract or two into place. Our shop front repair numbers are down for the past month."

"You're right. It's not looking all that great for us. Still, we have other prospects. Remember, I plan to go see a few of the local businesses this week and pass out our cards. There's the potential for a lot of new repair work if they decide to go with us."

"Over the bigger repair shops in town," I lament. "I'm not sure how likely that is if the local high school won't even give us a sniff. Shit."

My friend sighs for a third time and asks, "What's really eating at you, buddy?"

Stopping near a park bench and sitting down, I answer, "My wife is going to interview for a second job this afternoon."

"That's a good thing, right?"

"Not really," reply as I think about how I could possibly tell him about my wife's attempt to become a stripper on the weekends.

"What does that mean?"

"Well, let's just say that it's not the sort of job that I think she should be doing. We had a huge talk about it, though, and Lindsey is still going through with it."

"Oh. What sort of job is it again?"

My jaw flexes. "It's just one of those terrible side jobs that some bosses hire you for and then give you a lot of grief. Let's just say that it's not a great job."

"I got you," Jeff replies. "I've had some jobs in my life that made me want to roll over and die, but I saw them through. You should encourage your wife to be open about it and tell you when things get tough for her. That would be a lot better than just throwing her to the wolves on her own."

"Throwing her to the wolves?" The insinuation causes me to tense as I think about it. "I'm not throwing her to the wolves, Jeff."

"Oh? You sound like you're dead set against her taking this job, Braden. If she's going for it, she obviously knows that you both need the money. Be thankful that Lindsey is willing to do that for you both and support her."

Though I disagree with the job that my wife has chosen to go after, Jeff is right. I need to be more supportive of her than I have been recently. Lindsey is simply looking for a way to help us get the bills paid on time, and I can't fault her for that. She wants to help and we honestly need the help badly. It might be difficult to think about her naked in front of lots of horny men, but there's only so much we can do otherwise. I'll have to get over my prejudices against her working at a gentlemen's club.

"Thanks for the advice," I say to my old friend. "It really helps."

"Anytime, buddy." He pauses before saying, "I'll catch you on Monday at the shop. We'll plan for what the next steps will be then."

"See you later." We hang up and I get up from the seat where I've been sitting. I feel better now that I've spoken to Jeff about my situation with Lindsey. He's right about it all. She's trying to help and I need to be there for her in any way that I can. I *will* be there for my wife, no matter what happens with this second job. I owe her at least that much.

Chapter Five: Drawing a Crowd

Three weeks have gone by since Lindsey began her second job at the gentlemen's club, and I grow antsier by the day. My wife and I don't talk about her work there, and maybe that's a good thing in general, but I want to know more about it. Sure, she's stripping, but how much stripping is she actually doing? How many men are watching her each night? I have decided that tonight, a Saturday night, I will go into the club and watch her perform.

"Nice," I say as I look at myself in a mirror in the bathroom. An old baseball cap, a thin jacket, and some fake glasses that I found at a local consignment shop should work well to keep me hidden from Lindsey's eyes while she's on stage. "You're nuts," I tell myself with a chuckle as I turn and walk out of the bathroom and toward the front door of our house. It's a quick drive to the club, just fifteen minutes away once rush hour traffic has subsided. My heart quickens and my breathing becomes a bit shallower as I park toward the back of the lot.

"Ten dollars cover." I look at the man just inside the door and nod my head as I pull out the cash and hand it over. In turn, he motions me through a second door that leads me into the main room of the gentlemen's club.

The music is loud and lights are flashing as a cute blonde woman is moving up and down a pole on one of the three stages. I smile as I take a seat nearby, in good view of all three venues. Though there are no other women dancing at the moment on the other stages, there are ladies moving through the tables and chairs. Some sit on men's laps and whisper into their ears while others take drink orders. A petite red-head wearing a small pink mask over the top half of her face approaches me.

"Good evening, hot stuff. Can I get you anything tonight? Maybe a beer or a glass of whiskey?"

I shake my head. "Maybe later. I'm here in town for a visit and I thought I would come by and see what things are like at this club."

She smiles as she moves to where she is standing between my legs. "And do you like what you see so far?" Her blue eyes stare intently at me as she puts a hand on my shoulder and gently runs a finger over my neck.

"Well, um..." I find myself a little tongue tied as I smile back at her. I'm sure they are told to do this sort of thing to try to get their customers to spend more money on drinks and private dances.

"I can wait a while," she says before sitting down on one of my legs. Her soft, full breasts are peeking up over the teddy she is wearing, and I find it difficult to avoid looking directly at them instead of at face.

"Um, what's your name?" I ask as I try to start some kind of conversation with the young woman.

"Passion," she replies. "What's yours?" She runs a finger along my chest and I feel my cock begin to stiffen. Passion feels this happening against her thigh and she taps my bulge with her leg as she says, "Thank you."

"My name," I begin. "I'm Braden." My face suddenly flushes red as I realize I've used my real name. What if the woman on my lap has spoken to Lindsey about me and knows my name? Will she tell my wife that I've come here? Will she tell her that I got a hardon for her?

"It's very nice to meet you, Braden." She runs a finger along my neck once again, and then to my ear. She then begins to gently rub it as I feel myself become even more attracted to her. "Have you ever been to a gentlemen's club before?"

I smile uneasily. "Yeah, a few times. I don't tend to make it a habit, though."

Passion giggles. "I could tell that by the way you're so timid with me. Most experienced guests are right to the point with what they want when they come here."

"What they want?"

She nods her head. "Sure. Like a private dance or something like that." She leans closer to me and I can smell the aroma of her sweet perfume. Everything she is doing to me causes my body to yearn for her.

It wouldn't take much for me to fuck Passion in every way possible if given that chance. "A private dance for ten minutes is fifty bucks. But for you, I could go forty." The young woman leans toward me and kisses my ear before taking my earlobe into her mouth and sucking on it gently for a second or two. She then sits back up and smiles at me.

"Well...I can't right now," I say as I struggle to maintain what little composure I have left. "Someone is coming to meet me here and I don't want to miss him."

"A friend?" I nod my head to help complete the lie. "When he gets here I can dance for the both of you. Of course, I would love a nice tip, too."

"Of course," I say with a nervous chuckle. "I'll tell him when he gets here and then maybe we can work something out." My mind is racing with what to say or do next as I try to keep myself from making a huge mistake. If Lindsey were to discover that I've come here to see her perform, it might make things more difficult for the two of us. If she found Passion trying to seduce me into a dance or even something more, that would be even worse for me.

"I'll see you later then, alright?" I smile and nod as Passion gets up from my lap, winks at me, and then walks away to find another man to flirt with. By this time, the performer on stage has finished and an announcer begins to speak into a microphone.

"Ladies and gentlemen, welcome to Benton Gentlemen's Club. Tonight we have a special treat for you. Flame, our most popular dancer, will be with us in just five minutes. She will be taking center stage along with three other girls to present to you her first performance of the night. Please get ready for Flame!" Men in the audience clap, so I do the same as I watch a crowd of about a dozen more guys come in through the door and approach the center stage. One of them, a young man who appears to be in his early twenties, sits down near me.

"Hey, how are you tonight?" he asks me with a smile.

"Good," I reply. "You?"

He nods his head and continues to smile. "I'm great as long as I haven't missed the main act tonight."

"The main act?"

"Flame," he replies. "Didn't the guy just announce that she's up next?"

"Um, yeah. He said in about five minutes."

"Good." The man beams as he sits back in his seat and reaches into his pocket. He pulls out a roll of cash and holds it tightly in his hand. I'm a little taken aback by the move as I look from him to the others gathering in the gentlemen's club. There's hardly an open seat left as the lights dim and music begins to play.

"Ladies and gentlemen. May I present, *FLAME!*" The sixty or seventy people in the room, overwhelmingly of the male persuasion, cheer as a spotlight comes on and the other lights in the room go out. Soon, a curtain opens and three women in black teddies walk out and begin to dance around. A fourth one, wearing a mask over the top of her face just as the others are, follows and makes her way to the center pole.

"She always has backup dancers," the young man says as he stares at the stage. "But none of them are as beautiful as Flame." I turn and watch the performance as the toned, athletic woman in the middle swings around the pole as if it's second nature to her. Her movements are fluid and her dark brown hair tosses beautifully in large circles. I get hard as I watch her work, wondering who she really is. The mask covering the top half of her face disguises her very well as she gyrates on stage.

"What?" I focus my eyes on a small spot beside the crotch of her teddy. It's difficult to tell at first what it is as she moves around, but there's something familiar about it. "A *tattoo?*"

The man beside me hears me. "You can see it better when she's completely naked," he tells me. "It's a blue jackrabbit."

My heart pounds hard as my jaw drops and I realize who the masked woman really is. *"Lindsey?"* My wife works the pole like a true professional as the women around her slowly remove their gloves and teddies. They each show off their round breasts and perfect beavers of varying degrees of trim and baldness. However, I'm not as interested in them as I am in the woman in the red teddy as she teases her way out of her own outfit and soon stands completely naked before all of us. There's no doubt in my mind at this point that the woman is my wife.

My cock gets hard as she moves around the stage, posing in ways that causes her pussy lips to open wide so that the men surrounding the stage can see her beautiful clit and all that lies around it. As she does this, money is put on the stage before her and she collects it, folding and then sticking it into a small garter around one of her legs. Lindsey is showing her body off and it's having a real effect on my horniness.

"Here, baby," the young man beside me says. Lindsey walks over and crouches down so that she can play with her pussy while he watches. She then leans back and shows off her feminine wares as the man stares into her tightness. It seems as if he might reach over and touch her muff, but he doesn't dare as she gets back up and takes the ten dollars he has offered her. She smiles and then looks at me. I turn my face down so that my wife doesn't recognize me.

"Oh, come on, man. She likes you." The man beside me laughs as I fish into my pocket to retrieve five dollars. I put it on the stage and Lindsey takes it before moving on.

The show goes on for several more songs, with my wife occasionally kissing one of the women on stage or fondling them. My eyes, glued to the performance, take in the very thrill of the action before me. I wish so badly that I could follow Lindsey backstage and fuck her when she leaves. Though I probably could, I don't want her to know yet that I've come to watch her. She had made me promise that I wouldn't do this as it is.

Finally, after about ten minutes, Flame and her backup dancers leave the stage. "Give it up for Flame and her girls, ladies and gentlemen!" the announcer says as they exit the stage. At this point, other ladies come onto the side stages and begin to dance and strip.

"Once every hour," the young man nearby me says with a smile. "Are you sticking around for the next one? She might even do some tricks on stage."

"Tricks?"

"Yeah, like gripping the bar with her legs while she's upside down. Flame is really good at that." If I didn't know better, I might suspect that the man has it bad for Lindsey.

"Sounds like fun, but I have to go. I have an early day tomorrow." I get up from my seat and nod at the young man.

"See you around," he replies before going back to watching the other girls on the stage. I make my way back to the gentlemen's club entrance and then leave. I've seen what Lindsey is up to here and I don't need to see anymore. I also don't need to take the risk of having her know that I've come here after promising not to do so.

As I get into my car, I say to myself, "She was fucking hot, Braden." My cock getting hard again, I wonder where Lindsey learned to move and flirt the way she was doing while dancing. Is that story about the friend true or was it really her? I knew my wife in college for the last year, but who knows what she was up to before then? There's the distinct possibility that she was the one stripping for extra cash. No matter what the truth is, Lindsey is obviously a stripper now and a very good one. I have no doubt that there were dozens of hard cocks in that club tonight.

Chapter Six: Opportunity Awaits

I don't tell her at first, and it seems that Lindsey is completely unaware that I was at the gentlemen's club last night to see her dance and strip. Enjoying a cup of coffee while relaxing in the living room in front of the television, I eagerly await her to join me.

"Thanks for making coffee," my wife says as she has a seat nearby and puts her feet up. "It's getting tough for me to get out of bed on the days after I work at the club. I have to get to the spa in an hour, though." She moves around in her chair as she smiles over at me. "Did you get plenty of sleep last night? You were out of it when I got home."

Nodding my head, I reply, "I slept pretty well. How did last night go? Did you make any money?"

"I made very good money, Braden. I think it was more than I've made in any one night before. The manager gave me a couple hundred dollars as a bonus." She smiles broadly at me before taking another sip of her coffee.

"It sounds like you're making more at the club than at the day spa. Have you thought about quitting the spa?"

She raises an eyebrow. "Quitting the spa? That would be a little reckless, wouldn't it? I mean, I've only been working at the club for three weeks or so."

"Three very good weeks," I point out. "Apparently, Flame is a really popular girl there."

Lindsey sits forward in her seat, her eyes wide. "How do you know my stage name, Braden? I didn't tell you that."

I chuckle. "No, you didn't. I found out for myself last night." My cock becomes hard as I watch the changing expression on my wife's face. I can hardly believe that I've gone ahead and told her that I was there.

"We agreed that you wouldn't go!" she says with a nervous giggle. "Braden, you should have warned me that you were coming to the club."

"And then what? Would you have set me up with a girl for the evening?" I laugh as I shake my head. "No, I wanted to see you perform without worrying about me watching you. We both know that you get nervous very easily."

Lindsey's face turns bright red as she looks me over. "Braden, why? What did you expect to see when you showed up at the club?"

I move around in my own seat as I adjust my hardon. My beautiful wife's dark brown eyes penetrate deeply into my soul as we look at each other. I love her more now than ever and I suspect that she feels the same for me. However, seeing her perform for other men has changed something inside me. Before, I was jealous and didn't much like the idea of Lindsey sharing her body with others. Now, I feel as if I would be happy to share her in an even more intimate way with another man.

"I wanted to watch how other men reacted to you while you danced," I reply with a wicked grin on my face. "I wanted to see if they got horny because of you. And they did."

My wife blushes even more. "You liked other men seeing me, then?"

"I loved it. As a matter of fact, I would like for you to do more." My heart races as I begin to admit just how naughty my thoughts have become since last night. "I would love to know that you are doing things in the back room with other men for easy money."

Lindsey, appearing a little shocked, shakes her head. "I don't understand, Braden. Are you saying that you want me to do *sexual* favors for guys who are willing to pay for them?"

"Sure. Why not?" My cock is now at full staff and I feel as if I might come inside my pants. I have to move it around again to get comfortable in my seat. "You could make a lot more money that way."

She shakes her head. "The management doesn't like that sort of thing, though."

"But other girls do it anyway, right?"

"They sometimes do," she admits.

"Like what?" I press her so that I can imagine my wife doing those things with other men. I want her to *say* it.

"Um, well, you know. Hand jobs and oral stuff," Lindsey says as she looks away from me for a moment. "Just anything you could do in bed with a boyfriend or girlfriend."

"Full sex too?" My heart thumps hard inside my chest as I smile.

"Some girls do that," Lindsey confirms. "But if they were to get caught, they could go to jail and possibly lose their jobs at the club. The management doesn't want any problems with the police."

"That's understandable. But you know that you can get away with it as long as it happens in the back room, right?"

"There could be undercover police who try to bait girls into doing that, Braden. It's very dangerous."

"But most of the girls know who they are, right?" I've never gone to get a private dance from a girl at a gentlemen's club, but I've learned a lot from friends about how things generally work. The women are normally very particular about who they will take to a private room in the back, even requiring some men to buy a public lap dance first to make certain that they're not vice squad officers. Once they are sure of who they are dancing for, then they offer the more expensive option of going to the back for a few dances. This can be costly for the guy, but then again he might just get more than the standard dance. He might get lucky.

"Some of the ladies know," Lindsey says while nodding. Her dark eyes meet with mine again. "You would be okay with me doing that sort of thing with other men?"

"I would," I admit. "After seeing you last night, I think the earnings potential would be huge. You might even be able to quit your regular job and just work at the club, Lindsey. Wouldn't that be nice?"

She frowns. "Are you serious? You want me to whore myself out so that I can quit working at the day spa?"

"It's not *whoring* yourself out," I chuckle. "It's an economic opportunity. You could give hand jobs or blow jobs. It wouldn't have to be full sex, honey. Just some fun that will cause those men to put more money into your pockets. Besides, I've seen how they toss money at you on stage. I think it would be even better for you if you started taking some of them to the back room with you. Just touch them until they come, baby."

"Until they *come?"* My wife's face goes from bright red to pale as she puts her coffee cup down on a small table beside her chair. Never before in our marriage have I suggested that she do anything with another man sexually. I'm sure Lindsey is wondering why I've had the sudden change of heart on all this, and her thoughts about it are scary for her. Before last night, I was a kind, protective husband. Now I'm trying to convince her to play with other men's cocks.

"You can do it," I tell her. "Just think about the money. Don't you want to make that kind of money, Lindsey? Wouldn't it be nice?" Of course, there is a deeply greedy side to my way of thinking. We need the money. The more she can make, the better off we'll be. I'm willing to accept the idea of my wife sucking and even fucking a guy to make more money.

"I'll have to think about it," she tells me quietly. "That's not something I've really considered, Braden. It would be a huge change in our relationship."

"It's just business," I tell her. "We all have talents and we can use them in ways to make money. What you are doing and might do with other men is just the same sort of thing. You're using your talents to make money." My cock continues to pulsate inside my pants as I imagine what it will be like for Lindsey to put her lips around another man's shaft. I've had some fantasies in the past concerning just such a thing, but never have I seen it as a real possibility. "I want to know afterwards what you did with another man and what it was like," I say out of sheer horniness.

She shakes her head. "Braden, are you sure that's something you would want to hear about?"

"Yes, I would."

Lindsey turns her eyes toward me. "I don't know. That's a little weird, right? For me to *tell* you how I'm cheating behind your back?"

"You're not cheating, my love. Remember, it's just business. It's not cheating if I'm asking you to do it. There's nothing that will go on behind my back." I smile at my wife as my body quakes with anticipation. I really do want to know about her encounters with other men. I want to hear about a hand job or blow job that she's given some random guy at the club. I want to know if she *fucks* them.

"I don't know..."

"Fuck them too," I tell her as I pant hard. "Fuck as many as you can for as much money as you can." Pre-coming inside my pants, I move around to get my cock back to a comfortable position.

"Braden."

"Just fuck them hard, okay? The ones willing to pay, fuck them hard, baby. Show them how horny you can be." It's such a thrill to say this to Lindsey as I fantasize about her athletic body on top of another man's johnson. My wife can be a sexual tiger when she wants to be and I'm horny as I conjure these images inside my mind.

There is a brief silence between us as Lindsey considers what I've asked of her. She knows that something has snapped inside me and that things will never be the same between us. I desperately want her to give pleasure to other men and to collect money for doing so. It would likely be even more profitable than the dancing and stripping, but it would also require her to leave her comfort zone a bit more. Though I ask this of her, I get the feeling that Lindsey has already been considering this added work.

"I'll see what I can do," she finally says. "You *are* okay with this, right?" I nod my head. "If I do this, don't bring it up like I've cheated on you, Braden. It will never be fair game in arguments."

"Agreed," I answer quickly. "Look, I'm fine with the idea of you with other men, baby. I've been thinking about it and it's just for the money."

"But, what if I *enjoy* it?" she asks. The question surprises me.

"Um, well, work can be enjoyable, right?" It's the only response that I have to give such a question. She could *enjoy* it? Maybe she could, though I wasn't really considering that until she said something about it just now.

"Yes, it can," she agrees. Lindsey smiles at me as she picks up her coffee cup. "I guess I'll see about making more money that way, then. It might turn out to be the best thing I've ever done."

"Sure." I smile back at my wife and nod as I lift my coffee cup. I take a sip and realize that it's getting a bit cold. Getting up from my chair, I go to the kitchen to get a fresh cup. As I do, I think about Lindsey with other men and the money they will give her for her sexual services. My cock is still hard and I'm still horny for her. This is certainly about more than money to me now. It's about whatever gets me off.

Chapter Seven: Deep Pockets

I've been waiting patiently over the last week to hear from Lindsey as to whether she has taken any men to the back of the gentlemen's club for something more than just dancing and stripping. Though we have talked a little about it here and there, my wife has not indicated to me yet that she's done anything of the sort. She's nervous and afraid of what might happen and whether she might get caught in the act of doing something illegal. I understand that concern completely. However, I wish she would go ahead and do something with one or two other men and then tell me all about it.

"I need to talk to you." I look up, shocked to see Lindsey walking through the door of the computer repair shop.

"Hey, honey."

"Can we go to your office?" She appears a little shaken as she holds her hands together near her waist and fidgets a little.

I look over at Jeff. "Can you watch the front for a few?"

"Sure, buddy." He smiles at me and then says to Lindsey, "It's good to see you today."

"You too." Her eyes avoid contact with him as she walks past me toward the back of the shop. We go into the small office and my wife closes the door behind us, locking it.

"Okay, you've gotten my attention," I say with a chuckle. "What's up?"

"Last night," she begins while sitting down on the edge of my desk, "I did what you wanted at the club."

My cock stiffens. "You gave somebody a hand job?"

Lindsey pulls a roll of cash from her purse and lays it on the desk. "There's over a thousand dollars there, Braden."

"What?" I pick up the money and look at it. It's been a while since I've seen this much money in my hand at one time. "From last night?"

She nods her head. "Yeah, from last night. I did what you asked me to do. I gave a few guys hand jobs and even one of them a blow job." Her brown eyes look away from me.

"You put your *mouth* over another man's dick? *Shit.*" I pre-come a little as I smile. "Did he come inside your mouth?"

Lindsey looks at me as if I'm a complete moron. "He wouldn't have paid me if I hadn't let him, Braden. Yes, he came inside my mouth."

"Hot damn!" I can barely contain my excitement. I look at my wife's soft lips and imagine them hugging another man's rugged, stiff pole. I would give almost anything to have been able to see her blow the guy.

"You're happy with this? Braden, honestly, are you getting off on the thought of me doing this with other men?"

A mischievous grin fills my face. "Yes, my love. Like most guys would if they were in my position."

"You would." Lindsey grimaces. "I thought it was just about the money for you."

Nodding, I reply, "Of course it's about the money, Lindsey. But it's also something that happens to make me very horny. I love the fact that you have been helping other guys come."

"Wow." I guess my wife was really convinced that it was only about the money she could make as far as I was concerned. There are reasons for her belief. For one, I told her that it was just business. If that was true, then I wouldn't be so horny at the thought of her sucking off some other man. It's true, though I'm sure it might be hard for her to admit it; I am very happy that she sucked on another man's cock.

"A thousand dollars in one night for blow jobs and hand jobs?"

She shakes her head. "There was one other thing." Lindsey swallows hard as she once again fidgets around in the office. "One man asked for full sex, but I told him I couldn't do that. He even offered me a thousand dollars if I would go along with his request." My cock continues to throb as my wife tells me this. "I turned that down."

"For a thousand bucks? I'd have fucked him myself for that much," I chuckle. Lindsey frowns. She obviously isn't very happy with my comment.

"I didn't want to go that far," she tells me with a strained look on her face. Lindsey looks down and thinks for a moment before looking back up at me and adding, "But I did something that I'm a little embarrassed about."

"Embarrassed? In what way?"

My wife swallows hard. "I agreed to let him rub his dick on my pussy. We did that for a while and..." Lindsey's voice trails off as she looks away from me. She is apparently gathering her thoughts as my manhood continues to anticipate what she is about to tell me.

"Honey?"

"Yeah, okay." Lindsey nods her head and looks at me again. "I used his cock to rub my clit and we both came together." Lindsey folds her arms and looks down at the floor.

"You *both* came? As in, you both *orgasmed?"* I watch as she nods her head. "Shit, honey. Tell me what it was like. Don't leave anything out."

"It was embarrassing," she tells me for the second time. "It wasn't what I wanted to happen, but it did."

"Explain *how* it was embarrassing." My heart races as I watch the way Lindsey moves around in her seat. Her reaction to whatever happened has as much of an effect on me as the thought of her letting a man rub his cock on her pussy.

"It's just that..." Again, she pauses to think. "Well, I guess it's just the way I used his dick. I didn't ask him, I just took it from him and began to rub it on myself like it was a dildo or something. He didn't tell me to stop, so I kept going." Her dark brown eyes look at me for a fleeting moment before looking down again. I would have to guess that she's also studying how I am reacting to this information.

"You rubbed his cock on your pussy?" She nods. "And then?"

Lindsey licks her lips. "Then I kept going and I was getting so wet." Her face turns deep red. "He even told me that I was getting really wet. We were both getting closer and closer and then I suddenly came." My wife shakes her head while looking down at the floor. "Shit, I didn't think I could do that."

"Come?"

"No," she replies flatly as she looks up at me. "I...well, I..." It seems that my wife won't be able to get the words out at first, but she eventually finishes the sentence. "I squirted."

"Squirted?" I laugh. "Did you pee on the guy?"

"No, I *squirted.* A *lot.*" Her face turns an even deeper shade of red than before. "I didn't pee on him, Braden. Fuck. I think he might have thought that I did at first, though."

"Really?" I've heard of female ejaculation, but I've never actually seen it happen with anyone I've been with sexually. Did Lindsey ejaculate all over the guy? Damn, I wish I had seen her do it!

"It's embarrassing," she continues. "It got all over his balls and his stomach. He even jumped a little when I did it."

"Did he get off?"

"Yeah, he came right as I did. But he still jumped when I gushed all over him."

"So, not just a *little* squirt? A *gushing* of liquid?"

"Stop smiling," Lindsey says to me as she shakes her head. "You don't understand how embarrassing that was for me Braden. I've never done that with anyone before."

"Did he complain?" I ask with a laugh. "Seriously, did the guy tell you he was upset that you squirted all over him?"

Quiet at first, my wife replies, "He said that he liked it, but I can't see how anyone could like a woman doing that to them. It was a *lot* of fluid, Braden. That's never happened whenever we've had sex, has it?"

"No, honey, it really hasn't, but..."

"It's gross. A lot of it came out of me."

"You *ejaculated,*" I chuckle. "It's okay. Most men practically pray for that to happen with their wives and girlfriends. What you did was make that guy's day." Looking at the roll of cash on my desk, I ask, "How much of this was for that?"

Lindsey finally looks at me again. "He offered me a thousand for sex. Since we didn't have full sex, he gave me five hundred dollars for making a mess all over him. Mainly because I squirted."

"Bingo!" I laugh as I clap my hands together. I can only imagine what Jeff is thinking outside the door as he hears us talking in the office. Though it's difficult to pick up a full conversation through the office door, it's easy enough to hear people get excited while in here.

"You think it's funny?"

"No, Lindsey. I think it's sexy. *You're* sexy." I help my wife up to her feet and twirl her around so that she's facing the desk.

"What are you doing?" I pull her shorts down quickly, exposing her ass before pushing her over the edge of my desk. "Braden."

"You've turned me on," I tell Lindsey as I unfasten my pants and drop them to my feet along with my briefs. My cock already swollen, I wedge the head of it between her pussy lips and begin to rub it along her clitoris. "You fucking slut," I groan as I feel her little nub become hard and swollen.

"Shit, Braden," she whimpers at me. "This isn't the place to do this."

"Yeah it is." I push my shaft into her wet beaver, the feeling of its soft walls along my skin causing me to buck. It's been a while since I have wanted to fuck Lindsey so badly. The thought of her squirting all over the other guy makes me want to experience the same thing. "Your cervix," I mumble as I push deep into my wife and feel the hard, muscular ring. I move the head of my cock over it as I grip her ass with my hands tightly.

"Holy fuck, Braden," she groans as she pushes back against me. Her body is beginning to react as well. "You're turning me on." Lindsey reaches into her tight tee shirt and plucks at her nipples. My wife is so hot when she gets like this.

I thrust hard and fast as my small desk moves around inside the office. The squawking of the feet of the desk along the floor is loud and obnoxious while I enjoy fucking the love of my life. There's no doubt in my mind that Jeff can hear what's happening in here. I'm surprised that he hasn't tried to walk in through the locked office door to see what we're doing in here.

"Dammit, Braden! *Fuck!"* Lindsey bites her lower lip as I bounce into her hard cervix over and over again. Her ass acts as the perfect bumper pad for me as I collide with her.

"You're so fucking tight!" I growl at her. My balls ache for the release that is soon to come. "Dammit, Lindsey, I want to fill you with my jism!" I lift her feet off the floor for a moment as I get a little too carried away with thrusting.

"Braden...*OHHHHH!!!"* Lindsey squeals loudly as she begins to come. *"Ohhhh...UHHHHH!!!"* She suddenly begins to squirt, coating my cock and balls with her juicy wetness. I've not seen my wife do this before, so it becomes a huge focal point for me as I feel my own body begin to convulse with extreme pleasure.

"NAHHHH!!! Uhhhh...ohhhh...ohhhh...ohhhh..." I spurt hard inside her tight muff hole as Lindsey continues to squirt all over me. *"Ohhhh, fuck...ohhhh..."* Our bodies slap together hard, her soft ass taking the brunt of the collision forces between us. *"Fuck!"*

"Dammit...oh, Braden. Ohhhh..." We both finish squirting and spurting and I pull out of my wife's tight pussy. Some of my man sauce oozes out of her along with plenty of her own juices as it all drops to the floor. Together, we have made quite the mess and it satisfies me to see it.

"That was awesome," I chuckle as I look at Lindsey. She pulls her shorts up and just leans back against the wall.

She allows a half-grin as she looks over at me. "You didn't ask nicely, Braden."

"No, I didn't," I laugh. "But you didn't complain while you were climaxing, either."

"Touche," my wife replies with a giggle. "So, you really like that mess I've made all over you?" She nods toward my wet crotch.

"It's beautiful," I tell her. "Just beautiful."

"You'll have to clean yourself off," Lindsey continues. "And Jeff..." Her voice trails off. She has just reasoned out that he must have heard us fucking each other in the office.

"Yeah, Jeff," I say while nodding my head. "He'll not say anything to anyone else."

"He'll just talk to you about it, Braden. I'm so embarrassed." Her face turns red again in very much the same way it did as she told me about her customer at the club.

"Probably," I reply. "Still, he's a good guy. He won't push me too hard for information. I won't offer any." Reaching over, I take Lindsey's hand. "We both need to clean up, honey. I have some paper towels and tissues over there." I point toward a wall shelf. Looking down, I see my flaccid cock flex a little. Yes, I would screw my wife again if I thought I had the ability to recover so quickly. As it is, I'll have to spend the rest of the day just recalling what has happened here. I'll also be thinking about my wife with the stranger at the club last night. I want to see her do this with other men instead of just hearing about it. Maybe there is some way that I can convince her to go along with such an idea. This is soon to become my passion.

Chapter Eight: Looking Up

"Hey, man," Jeff says as I walk through the door of the computer repair shop. "Good to see you this morning."

I smile. "Good to see you, too." I make my way to the back counter where a coffee pot with fresh coffee is waiting for me. After pouring myself a cup, I turn and lean against the counter to take the first sip. Jeff continues to stare at me, an impish grin on his face. "Okay, spill it," I say with a chuckle.

Jeff sighs. "I noticed that you knocked a few things around in the office yesterday," he begins. "Messy, messy, messy." He continues to allow a smile to crease his face as I realize what he's talking about.

"Look, we made out a little," I lie. "You know how couples can be sometimes."

My business partner nods his head. "Sure I do. My wife can be the same way...in the bedroom." He laughs as he shakes his head. "You two were like a couple of horny college kids in there." My face turns bright red and becomes hot. I've never spoken to Jeff about anything remotely sexual before, and here he is commenting on my horniness with my wife.

"I told her you would be cool about that, Jeff. Don't make a liar out of me."

"Cool about it? I don't mind, just so long as you wipe things down when you're finished. Did you wipe everything down, Braden? I don't want to find any crusty stuff on the desk when I sit down to balance the books." He laughs again, this time even harder as he sees my reaction to his question.

"Sheesh, Jeff. Really?"

"Ah, I'm just playing with you, buddy. I know that you need to blow off a little steam once in a while. We all do." He continues, "Just tell Lindsey that I understand and I hope the bruising is gone soon."

"Fuck." We both laugh hard. My old friend enjoys making fun of anything that I do, especially when it might be the least bit embarrassing. We do this sort of thing to each other all the time. It's what sometimes pisses my wife off about him.

"Hey, some good news," Jeff says after calming down. "I called Bradley Lake School District again. They might be willing to allow us to work on their high school tech lab next month. They're doing some upgrades and need additional people to get everything set up and running before the fall semester begins."

I smile widely. "That would be an easy job. How much are they willing to pay?"

"Thirty dollars per unit," he replies.

I frown. "A little low, isn't it?"

"But they have a huge tech lab. Fifty computers and peripherals. They are also willing to pay another thousand dollars once the job is done."

"Twenty-five hundred dollars," I say with a nod. "Not great, but good. I can knock that out in a long day." Thinking for a moment, I tell Jeff, "Lindsey has been earning some extra money on the side as well. We've paid off most of our little bills and now we're working on the big ones."

"Wow. Very nice." Jeff asks, "She's making that extra money at the day spa?"

I shake my head before really thinking through my response. "Um, well, she has a second job that is working out really well for her."

"A second job? The one she interviewed for? Doing what?" My face again turns red as Jeff asks me this question. I've thought a lot about what I might say to him if he ever found out about Lindsey's side job at the gentlemen's club, but I haven't come up with a good answer just yet. I can't tell him the truth, though. I would never live it down.

"She's doing some consulting work," I reply. "You know she has a college degree, right? Well, she's working with another business in a consultant capacity."

Jeff raises an eyebrow. "Which company?"

Fuck. Why does my old friend have to be so damned inquisitive? For as long as I've known him, he's been this way whenever we have talked about anything. Though it can be annoying, I often answer every little question he has and then move on with my day. How do I answer this? I can't just tell him that Lindsey is stripping at a gentlemen's club as well as giving some guys a little something extra in the back room. Jeff would freak out. He would never drop the subject and my wife would hate me for telling him. No, I can't tell my business partner the truth. I need to offer him yet another lie.

"I'm not allowed to say," I begin with a smile. "Linsey is under contract with the business to keep things quiet. They don't want the general public to know what they are needing a consultant for."

"Oh, come on, buddy. I'm not the general public. I'm your good friend. You can tell me."

"Jeff," I say as I pat him on the shoulder. "I can't tell you. Lindsey made me swear to keep it quiet, even to you or anyone else I know."

"But, you can *trust* me." He raises an eyebrow as he posits, "She's not a prostitute or anything like that, is she?"

Goosebumps suddenly erupt along the back of my neck and both arms. *"No!* Why would you ask something like that?" I try to feign outrage as I shake my head and wave my hands around. "Geez, Jeff. She's my *wife,* not some common street hooker."

"I never said she was a *street* hooker," he says with a laugh. "She's making good money, right? It's just my filthy mind, man. Just ignore my whole thought process." Jeff is obviously joking around with me, but he's too close for comfort in his guessing. If he only knew the whole truth about what Lindsey has been up to.

"She's just very private in what she's doing in her consulting business," I tell him. "It's contractual." In an effort to move the conversation along, I say, "It's good that we have the school thing lined up, though. Hopefully we can get some more jobs in the near future."

"Working on it," Jeff says as he settles down on a stool nearby. "I've called several businesses in the area and offered to give a discount if they will use us as their preferred tech shop. Some of them seem very open to the idea. We actually have a couple of personal customers who work for those businesses and have given us great references. I think we'll get more work very soon."

"Great." I smile as I continue to think about my wife and what she is doing at the gentlemen's club three evenings each week. She has promised to somehow involve me a bit more in what she is doing, but I'm not sure how that will work. It would be weird for me to go to a back room at the gentlemen's club to watch Lindsey with another man.

The front door of the computer shop opens and a man walks in. He is carrying a small laptop that he places on the front counter. "Good morning."

"Good morning, sir," Jeff says as he turns around on his stool. "How can we help you today?"

"Well, this thing isn't turning on, even though it's fairly new."

"Ah, the new laptop. The Xao Delta Pro." I look over at my business partner. We have talked some about the new Chinese-made laptop that appears to have some very serious hardware issues. "It's likely one of the processor chips," I tell the man.

"How much does something like that cost to repair?" He grimaces as he looks at the laptop. There's no doubt in my mind that he is disappointed that he purchased the computer at all. However, when a laptop is overhyped in television commercials, people tend to flock to the store to buy it.

"A couple of hundred dollars, if that's all that there is wrong with it."

"Wow. I gave twenty-five-hundred dollars for it." He shakes his head. "Don't go over four hundred on it, okay? If it's a bigger repair, call me first and I'll decide what to do then."

"No problem." I nod over to Jeff as he begins to fill out the paperwork for the man. I leave the laptop on the counter top and make my way to the office before closing the door behind me. The smell of sex from yesterday still lingers thickly in the air.

"No wonder he knows," I say to myself as I look at the off-center desk and the carelessly tossed papers on top of it. Lindsey and I had a fun moment here and Jeff probably heard every bit of it. He knows what we did in the office together. He's not a complete fool, after all.

My phone buzzes inside my pocket and I pull it out to read a text message from my wife. "Tonight, Braden, don't be late coming home. I'll have a surprise waiting for you."

"A surprise?" I text back to her. "What surprise?"

"Just get home on time tonight. It's really important that you do this, Braden. Promise me."

"Okay," I reply. "I'll try."

"Don't try, just do it," she commands in the next message she sends to me. "I've set something up and it has to happen right then. Be home on time!" Lindsey also sends several angry face emojis in her message.

"Okay, honey, I will." I laugh to myself as I look down at my phone screen. My wife often tires of my refusal to commit to something such as a time to get home.

"Good. Be here." She ends her messages to me and I slide my cell phone back into my pocket. I wonder what she has planned for this evening? Lindsey rarely demands that I be home on time for anything.

"Hey, Braden," I hear Jeff say as he pokes his head in through the door of the office. "This guy's laptop is on the back counter for you. He wants it by Wednesday if that's cool."

Nodding, I reply, "Yeah, I'll get it knocked out sometime today. Hopefully it's just one processor and nothing any more costly."

"Hopefully so." Jeff turns and goes back to the front of the shop as I continue to allow my mind to ponder what my wife has in mind for this evening. Maybe she has a nice dinner and sex planned for the two of us? That would be great. My cock stiffens as I think about burying it deep inside her wet pussy. Lindsey is a sexy woman and a great fuck. Any time with her is a special occasion, especially now that I know she can squirt. If that's her plan, tonight should be really fun.

Chapter Nine: A Happy Customer

Lindsey moves nervously about the living room as I watch her. I'm home on time, but there's no dinner waiting and nothing has been said about us having sex. Disappointed, I'm beginning to think that maybe my wife never intended to fuck me tonight.

"What's got you so bothered?" I ask as I watch her pace the floor.

"It's past time," she replies without looking at me. "Dammit, I said six o'clock." She stops to look at the small clock on the wall before shaking her head. "Ten minutes late."

"Late? For what?" I move around in my chair as I frown. The lack of sexual attention from my wife is beginning to irritate me a little.

Lindsey finally stops and turns to look at me. "It's a surprise."

"Okay." I'm confused, but I try to go along with what's happening. "I'm surprised that we're sitting here and that I know nothing about what's going on."

My wife, frustrated with whatever is supposed to happen, looks hard at me. "You will owe me after this, Braden. You really will." I continue to be confused as she begins to pace the floor once again. Just as I begin to ask her something, there is a knock at the front door. She moves quickly to open it and greet the man on the other side. "Clint! You're a little late."

"I'm sorry," the tall, handsome young man replies as he walks into our home. I stand to my feet as I watch this stranger hug my wife.

"Um, okay?"

"Braden, this is Clint." I walk up to him and shake his hand while looking him over and wondering what he's doing in my house.

"Hello, Clint."

"Hello." He seems a little bashful as he looks from me to Lindsey.

"Clint will be joining me for a session in the bedroom and you will be watching."

"A *session?*" Suddenly, I realize what my wife has planned and why I will owe her later for this. "Really? Right *now?*"

"Right now," she replies as she takes the young man's hand and guides him toward our bedroom. I follow just behind them, surprised at the fact that Lindsey is actually going to go through with what I have been asking her to do. She is going to have a little fun with Clint while I watch them together.

"Traffic was really terrible," Clint offers as an excuse as we walk into the bedroom. Lindsey has him sit down on the end of the bed. I take a spot in a chair nearby.

"It's okay," my wife replies as she walks toward the bathroom. "I'll be right out." She closes the door behind her and I find myself alone with Clint.

Looking over at him, I can see why he's such an attractive client for my wife. He's well over six feet tall, has light brown hair and blue eyes. His body is that of an athletic man. Clint obviously takes time each day to work out, which is more than I can say for me. Lindsey is going to do something with the young man tonight, and I wonder if it will include full sex or just something close to it.

The bathroom door soon opens and my wife steps out. She's wearing a teddy that is similar to the one she wears on the dance stage at the gentlemen's club. Reaching over, Lindsey taps a button on her Alexa device and soon there is a sensual song playing in the room. My cock hardens as I watch her walk over to Clint and begin to gyrate in front of him.

"I'm so happy that you made it over, Clint." She runs her hands over his shoulders while smiling at him. My guess is that she has danced for him before, but that this is likely the first truly private dance she has given him.

"Me too," he says nervously as she runs her fingers along the sides of his face and smiles. "Thank you for inviting me..." Lindsey puts a finger along his lips.

"Just sit back and enjoy it all, big guy." Her brown eyes turn to me as she smiles and turns to show the young man her nice, round ass. She then drops down to his lap and begins to grind into him. It obviously has the intended effect as Clint takes a deep breath and grips the edge of the bed tightly.

"Wow," he says quietly as my wife then turns and faces him, her covered breasts in his face. She reaches behind her and unties the long string, soon allowing the top to fall down just a little. Lindsey catches it in her arms as she covers her beautiful mounds. My wife flirts with Clint a little as his eyes grow wide. What a tease she has become over the last few weeks!

"Here, sweetie," she finally says to him as she allows the top of her teddy to drop into his lap. Her sweet breasts are now for him to visually take in as she moves close to him. Lindsey presses them to either side of his face, pushing his nose and mouth into her wonderful chest valley. I reach into my pants and pull out my cock as it pre-comes, rubbing the slippery juice into the head of it as I watch the two of them together.

"You smell so nice," he tells her as she backs away a little. Clint kisses one of her breasts before taking a nipple into his mouth. Lindsey's athletic body shudders as she enjoys the feeling of his lips around her areola. I continue to move my hand over my shaft as I watch the two of them together.

Lindsey pulls Clint's face closer to her chest once again. Closing her eyes, she smiles as he enjoys sucking and licking her nipple. "That's nice," she moans quietly as she runs her hands through the young man's hair. I've fantasized about what it would be like to see my wife with another man like this, but actually seeing it is so much better than the way I had imagined it before.

This goes on for some time before Lindsey stands up and begins to dance again, her C-cup breasts moving with her as she shimmies and shakes in front of Clint. Leaning back, my wife uses her fingers to pull her teddy crotch to the side and play with herself, the young man is smiling and licking his lips as he watches her do it. He doesn't wait for long before reaching forward and helps to pull down the rest of her teddy, causing it to drop to the floor. I almost come as he bends down to sniff her twat.

"You can eat it," Lindsey says as she moves closer to him. He bends down and laps eagerly at her puffy, waxed beaver, causing my wife to buck a little. She puts her hands on his head and then runs her fingers through his hair. "You're good at this, big guy," she tells him as he enjoys the flavor of her nether region.

"Holy fuck," I moan as I pre-come some more. My cock is hard and pulsating and I want to get off so badly, but I know better than to do it so quickly. No, I'll wait to come when the lovers do. It will be so much better as I imagine being somehow tangled up in the midst of the two of them.

"Ah..." Clint pushes a finger into my wife's wet vagina and begins to finger her as she squeals a little. *"Oh..."* She reaches down to apparently control what he's doing a little better, but then she stops. Is he massaging her G-spot? That's my guess as I watch him play with her pussy. Lindsey bites her bottom lip and grinds into his hand as he digitally fucks my wife.

"You're so wet," he tells her as he leans forward and takes her other nipple into his mouth. This causes Lindsey to quake and move around a bit more with her hands on the young man's shoulders. Clint appears to be very knowledgeable as he pleases my wife.

Lindsey pulls away from him and helps him to his feet. She nimbly unfastens his pants and pulls them to the floor along with his underwear. My wife then kneels before him and puts her hand on his large phallus. "You really are a big guy, huh?" she says before kissing the tip of his swollen dick. His muscular body reacts, his hands coming down to rest on the top of her head. My wife opens her mouth and slowly takes in the meaty shaft before her.

"Fuck," he moans as he feels her lips hugging the sides of his pole. "Damn, you're so fucking good at this, Flame." I had forgotten that she goes by this stage name until hearing it from him just now. Smiling, I pull

hard on my engorged member, producing yet more pre-come for me to rub into it.

"Ack..." My wife gags a little as she forces the entire length of his hardness to the back of her throat. Lindsey can be a dedicated giver of oral sex when she really wants to be. *Lop...lop...lop...slurp...* Her mouth is juicy as she pleasures the young man in front of her. Her eyes closed, my wife works him over like the professional dick sucker that she is.

"Oh, shit, *stop!"* He pushes her away as he spurts a little. "I'm going to pop if you keep going," Clint informs her. "Please, slow down."

She smiles as she stands up. "Then lay down on the bed, big guy." Lindsey watches as he takes off the rest of his clothes before laying down. His large cock wags from side to side as he settles on top of the covers and waits for her. Lindsey joins him on the bed and straddles his manhood before lowering her body toward it. My wife's tight muff begins to swallow Clint's fleshy stick.

"Oh, yeah..." he moans as he feels Lindsey's moist tightness beginning to envelop his shaft. "That's what I want. *Fuck, yeah."* His face red, he reaches up and puts his hands on her round breasts. I can see why he came so close to losing it just a moment ago. My wife is the hottest woman in town. At least, that's my opinion. I honestly might have lost my wad with her earlier than he has if I were the one she was doing this with.

"You're really thick," she tells her client. "I like thick cocks, Clint. Do you like my pussy?" Lindsey leans back and puts her hands on his knees as she works her bare pussy up and down along his pole.

"I love your pussy," he grunts. "Can I come inside you? Please?"

My wife smiles. "That's another two hundred, Clint. Are you willing to pay for it?" He nods his head and smiles as Lindsey begins to move her vagina up and down his meat. "Okay, then. You can come inside me if you want." My wife reaches up and pulls her hair back for a moment as she moves slowly up and down on him. I nearly come as I see her do this with Clint.

"You're a fucking tease," I tell her as I masturbate. "A real fucking tease." Lindsey looks at me and just smiles before closing her eyes and continuing to fuck Clint.

"Oh, you're so tight," he moans while playing with her nipples. "So fucking tight. I wish I could fuck you all the time, Flame. I would fuck you all the time if you were my girlfriend."

She giggles. "You couldn't handle me *all* the time, Clint. Besides, it would be too expensive for you." Lindsey grinds hard into him, causing him to grit his teeth and moan as she does. I'm sure by now that the tip of his dick is rubbing against her firm cervix. My wife's cervix feels great on the end of a cock during sex.

"I can't wait to come with you, Clint. I might even squirt." It's the first time I've heard her speak about squirting as a positive thing. It is, of course, but for some reason Lindsey felt embarrassed about it when we discussed it earlier.

"Fuck, you can *squirt?!*" His face contorts as he smiles a little. "Wet me down, Flame. Fuck, I want you to wet me down!" Clint's ass grinds into the bed as Lindsey moves a little faster on top of him. Their bodies are now fully engaged in what they're doing and I can see that it won't be very long before they go over the coital cliff. I intend to go right along with them as I feel my balls ache for release.

"Clint," my wife moans as she leans back even further. One of her hands moves to her pussy, her fingers massaging her clit as the man's johnson slides in and out of her quickly. "Oh, fuck, clint. Come inside me, okay? I want to feel you blast your jism inside me. Blast me really hard." Her toned body moves up and down, landing hard on top of the young man each time. The smell of sex and the sound of flesh pounding together fill the room.

"I'm about to come," he says as his body becomes stiff. "I'm going to come...I'm...*coming...*" Clint suddenly thrusts his pelvis forward very hard, causing the sound between their colliding bodies to become much louder. *"Nahhh...uhhhh...uhhhh..."* His face turns bright red as he releases spurt after spurt of man sauce deep inside Lindsey's tight pussy. *"Ohhh...uhhhh...uhhhh..."* I envy him as he feels my wife's soft, moist cunt around his cock.

"OHHHHH, FUUUCCCCKKKKK!!!" Lindsey leans forward and begins to orgasm hard as well while her lover helps to thrust his cock deep into her. Her pussy, full and red, begins to squirt all over the man's crotch, legs, and the bed. *"UHHHHH!!! FUCK!!!"* My wife thrashes like a ragdoll on top of Clint as she orgasms hard. I don't think I've seen her come so hard in my life. Lindsey is unhinged as she finishes up with her lover on our bed.

"SHIT!" The first spurt from the end of my cock is powerful as it launches away from me and hits the side of the bed nearby. *"Dammit...fuck...oh, fuck...fuck..."* I pull hard on my phallus as I empty into my hand as well as onto the bed and floor below. I've masturbated plenty of times in my life, but I've never come like this before while working on myself. *"Fuck...what a mess..."* I soon push my cock back into my pants before turning to look at the two other people in the room.

"Braden," Lindsey says with a tired smile as she rolls off Clint. "I can't believe that you did that. You hate to come like that."

"Not really," I reply. "I needed to get off, and this was the best way to do that."

"Worth it," Clint finally says as he sits up and leaves the bed. "Damn, that was one hell of a ride." He pulls his wallet from his pants and opens it up. After pulling out several large bills, he hands them to my wife. "Thank you, Flame. This was so much more fun than just a private dance."

Lindsey leaves the bed and goes to him. After kissing the young man deeply, she replies, "You were so good, sweetie. We'll have to do this again very soon."

"Yeah, we will." He smiles at her and then turns to collect and put on his clothes. After he does this, I accompany him to the door and he leaves our home.

I walk back into the bedroom. “Damn, honey.”

Lindsey smiles. “Did you like the surprise I gave you?”

I smile at her. “I loved it. I’m a little shocked that you would actually do it, but I loved it. Thank you.”

“There are more men interested,” she tells me with a wicked smile. My wife then turns and walks into the bathroom before closing the door behind her. My spent pecker suddenly comes back to life as it hardens.

“More men,” I say to myself with a smile. One could only be so lucky.

Chapter Ten: No More Worries

"You know, I don't think you could have convinced me just three months ago that you would do what you have done," I tell Lindsey as we sit in the park and relax with our mocha caramel lattes. "It has been a real surprise for me."

She smiles as she turns to focus her dark brown eyes on me. "It's been a bit of a surprise for me too, Braden. Clint was..." My wife stops for a moment, smiling and looking down at her hot beverage as she does. "He was really into me, wasn't he?"

I chuckle. "I think you were into *each other* honey. As a matter of fact, I think you really enjoy what you are doing now. The gentlemen's club, dancing, having sex with customers..."

"Hey," Lindsey says with a laugh as she interrupts me. She reaches over and takes my hand. "Is it wrong of me to want to have sex with other men besides you? It worries me that you might begin to feel a little jealous of what I'm doing. I don't want that to happen, Braden."

"Baby, you saw what I did in that bedroom when you and Clint were having sex, right? I don't think I was really bothered by it at all. I had to clean up my own mess."

She nervously smiles and nods. "Sure, you were horny and you went along with it that night, but there will be other men, Braden. Some of these guys will want something at the club and they won't want to come home with me so that you can watch what we do. How will that affect you in the long term when that happens?" Lindsey is obviously very concerned for me and how our marriage will fare if she continues in her new line of work with her clients. I have thought a great deal about how easy it once was for me to become jealous if some guy were to so much as look at my beautiful wife. But something has changed for me over the last few weeks. I no longer see myself as a jealous husband. I see myself as a partner in all this, excited to see where Lindsey ends up from day to day with her clients and lovers.

"I can't promise you how I'll feel in a few months or years, but I know that I love what you're doing right now. Lindsey, you are free to do this without worry that I'll somehow blow up or become upset with you in the least. I want you to have fun with these other men. Sure, I'll want to know what you're doing with them, but I think that will actually keep me from becoming jealous of what you're up to. Please don't think that I'm about to change my mind about this and cause any stress between us."

Lindsey smiles as she pulls her medium ponytail behind her shoulder. "You really are an amazing husband, Braden. I've known that since we first got married. No matter what we have done in our married life together, you have always been sweet and loving to me. I really do appreciate that." My wife leans toward me and gives me a soft kiss on the cheek. Goosebumps rise along my neck as I feel her lips press against my bare skin. I love the feeling of my beautiful lover against me in such an affectionate way. It's easy to see why other men desire my wife so much.

"You've always been the perfect wife for me, my beautiful girl. You will always be perfect as far as I'm concerned, no matter what you do or who you are with. Just be ready to tell me all about what you have done with your clients if you can't get them to come over here to do things with you while I watch." My cock stiffens a little as I think about Lindsey with more men. Clint was fun, but I'm willing to bet that there are likely other guys out there who are more adventurous than even he was with my wife.

"Sure thing, sweetie." We get up from our seats in the park and begin to walk in the cool breeze of the early Sunday morning. I love Lindsey and I know that she loves me too. There is a desire between us that will always be hot and intense, regardless of what may happen at the gentlemen's club or in our bed between my wife and other men. This is just the beginning of our shared fantasy together. With a little planning and her time at the gentlemen's club, Lindsey and I will enjoy a lot more of a newfound hobby over the coming months. I can't wait to see what the next chapter in all this will bring the two of us. I'm excited, and I know the love of my life is too.

THE END

Don't miss out!

Visit the website below and you can sign up to receive emails whenever Karly Violet publishes a new book. There's no charge and no obligation.

https://books2read.com/r/B-A-GIXE-GDTQB

BOOKS 2 READ

Connecting independent readers to independent writers.

About the Author

Sign up to my mailing list to receive the two free epilogues for 'A Hotwife Adventure' and 'Hotwife Training' and to stay up to date on all of my latest releases! http://eepurl.com/c3ICWf Sign up to my Patreon account and receive exclusive Hotwife stories every month and sexy scenes every week! https://www.patreon.com/karlyviolet

Read more at https://www.patreon.com/karlyviolet.

About the Publisher

www.ingramcontent.com/pod-product-compliance
Ingram Content Group UK Ltd.
Pitfield, Milton Keynes, MK11 3LW, UK
UKHW041821200726
13854UKWH00001BA/432